HORSE TAILS b
MOOKIE the MUSTANG

MW00987024

Written by
Patricia Probert Gott

Illustrated by
Brenda Ellis Sauro

Published by PRGOTT BOOKS

P O Box 43, Norway, Maine 04268

WWW.PRGOTTBOOKS.NET

Horse Tails by Mookie the Mustang

Written by Patricia Probert Gott
Illustrations by Brenda Ellis Sauro
Layout by Laura Ashton

The Mustang

Wild as the eagle soaring above,
a mustang watches over his domain
proud,
majestic,
free.

Copyright © 2009 by Patricia Probert Gott

All rights reserved. No part of this work may be
reproduced or transmitted in any form or by any means,
electrical or mechanical, including photocopying and
recording, or by any information storage or retrieval
system, except with written permission from the
author. You may contact www.prgottbooks.net
or P. O. Box 43, Norway, Maine 04268

Hello, my name is Mookie. A man and woman named Bob and Amy love and care for me. My stable mate and lifelong friend is Rocky. We live on a farm in the country and go trail riding together in the woods. I have a stall of my own. I am well fed and have all the water I want to drink.

However, life was not always so easy.

You see I was born a wild mustang on land set aside in the West for horses to roam free—no corrals, no fences. I have a dark gray body with black legs, ear tips, mane and tail. A funny dark stripe down my back is a special trait handed down from my Spanish relatives. My color and type of markings are called "grullo".

My mother Goldie was a pretty palomino. She was the color of shiny gold and had a long white mane and tail. She had a soft nose that she used to nuzzle me with love or push me to go faster when we needed to move to safety in a hurry.

My father's name was Macho. He was dark brown with black legs, mane, tail and a dorsal stripe like mine. He was our family leader and protector. He would whinny loudly to warn us to run from the danger of predators. With his ears pinned back and his neck snaked out, he would circle our family and drive us to a different grazing area if other horse groups, called bands, came too close.

There were nine of us in Macho's band of horses. There were three mother horses or mares, a yearling boy-colt, a yearling girl-filly, and three of us baby horses, called foals. Rocky, a brown colt, and Speck, a small reddish filly, were my playmates.

During the summer months, we grazed on yummy green grass that grew in high mountain meadows. We foals kicked, bucked and chased each other. We played king of the mountain, rolled in the dust to scratch our bug bites, and took naps in the warm summer sun.

My most fun was pawing and splashing in deep water holes. However, by late summer they began to dry up. From then on, we would have to travel many miles to find small pools of drinking water. Mother would not allow me to splash around when water became scarce.

Our family shared the few remaining water holes with other horses and animals like elk, deer, and bighorn sheep.

I met and befriended Buddy, a young Bighorn sheep, called a lamb.

We were having a good nose-to-nose talk until our moms interfered. My mom flattened her ears and bared her teeth as Buddy's mother lowered her head and pawed the ground.

"Baa, nice to meet you," Buddy said as he scampered back to his mother.

I was exploring some large rocks one day when I heard a rattling sound. I began sniffing to find the noise when suddenly my father Macho appeared.

"You must keep away from rattlesnakes," he warned as he nipped me on my rump driving me back to the safety of the band.

As the weather turned cold and snow fell on the high ridges, we grazed for grasses on lower mountain slopes. It kept getting colder, and when snow covered the low valleys we ate sagebrush, bark, and pawed in the snow for dead grass and dried weeds.

We were hungry much of the time.

Finally, spring arrived bringing much water from the melting snow. Our horse band wandered back up to high plateaus searching for newly sprouted plants and grasses.
I was now a year old.

As the weather turned warm, my new baby sister was born. She looked very funny to me as she tried to stand on her long wobbly legs. Her color was pale yellow with a dorsal stripe and dark legs like mine. She had a short black mane, and a stubby tail that always moved.
I named her Swish.

The first flakes of snow fell early that year and it was a long cold winter. Food for our family was scarce. In the spring, Macho looked very thin and he laid down a lot.

A large black father horse known as a stallion came to visit our family one day. He fought with Macho and chased him away. My mother said the black stallion, named Sage, would be our new leader.

Sage was not friendly to Rocky and me. He laid his ears back whenever we came near. One day he reared and threatened to kick us. We scampered away.

Rocky and I joined two other young stallions, Booker and Toto, forming a bachelor, all-boy horse group. Sometimes we stayed close to our old family. Sometimes we wandered off on our own. We were young, strong and healthy. We raced the wind whenever we wanted and explored mountaintops, valleys and canyons.   What fun we had!

We followed a trail through an area thick
with fir trees early one morning on our way to
water. I first saw it—then heard it—"Grrr,"
it growled from a ledge. It was a mountain
lion! I whinnied loudly to warn my friends of
danger and we ran to the water hole where
the other horses were gathered.

That fall something happened that changed my life forever. Metal flying machines called helicopters rounded up our bachelor group and my old family, along with several more horse bands, and drove us into a large corral.

The running and racing excited me. The corral worried me. I was relieved to meet my mother and sister there. I felt safe again.

Horse doctors, called vets, checked all the horses in the corral for injuries. As I took my turn in the chute, a man gave me shots against flu, tetanus, and rabies. Then someone drew numbers on my neck so I would never be lost. The numbers told my color, markings and year of birth.

I ate hay and drank water in the corral where I stayed for several days. Then Bob and Amy adopted Rocky and me. They loaded us into a horse trailer and hauled us many miles to their farm in the East.

Since arriving here, I have lived happy and content. I am very lucky to have them for my owners and I hope to remain here forever.

However, I will always be proud to be a mustang from the West.

The End

Can't Wait for More?

Watch for other books in the

HORSE TAILS series

www.prgottbooks.net

The next title in the series:

"Horse Tails by
Horses In Harness"

8025683R0

Made in the USA
Charleston, SC
01 May 2011